Table of Contents

Rourke
Educational Media
rourkeeducationalmedia.com

Can you find these words?

feast

harvest

Natives

Pilgrims

The First Thanksgiving

Pilgrims

The **Pilgrims** left England.
They sailed to another land.

People lived on the land.
They were called **Natives**.

They helped the Pilgrims.

The Pilgrims learned to plant corn.

They learned to plant beans.

They had a **harvest.**

harvest

They had food for the winter.

The Pilgrims and Natives were thankful.

feast

They had a **feast.**

The feast lasted three days.

This was the first Thanksgiving.

Did you find these words?

They had a **feast**.

They had a **harvest**.

They were called **Natives**.

The **Pilgrims** left England.

Photo Glossary

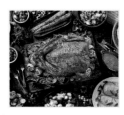 **feast** (feest): A meal with lots of food and drinks.

 **harvest** (hahr-vest): The season when crops are gathered.

 **Natives** (nay-tivs): People who lived in a place before outsiders arrived.

 **Pilgrims** (pil-gruhms): The group of people who left England to go to America in 1620.

Index

About the Author

Terri Fields loves reading with and writing for children. When she's not reading or writing, she likes walking on the beach.

© 2019 Rourke Educational Media

www.rourkeeducationalmedia.com

PHOTO CREDITS: Cover: ©DNY59; p.2,10,14,15: ©LauriPatterson; p.2,8,14,15: ©Pierre Desrosiers; p.2,4,14,15: ©Science History Images/©Alamy Stock Photo; p.2,3,14,15: ©North Wind Pictures Archives/©Alamy Stock Photo; p.6: ©venturecx; p.7: ©tab1962; p.12: ©GL Archive/©Alamy Stock Photo.

Edited by: Keli Sipperley
Cover and Interior design by: Rhea Magaro-Wallace

Library of Congress PCN Data
The First Thanksgiving / Terri Fields
(Time to Discover)
ISBN (hard cover)(alk. paper) 978-1-64156-206-5
ISBN (soft cover) 978-1-64156-262-1
ISBN (e-Book) 978-1-64156-310-9
Library of Congress Control Number: 2017957904

Printed in the United States of America, North Mankato, Minnesota